Born to Read

Story by
JUDY SIERRA

Pictures by
MARC BROWN

Alfred A. Knopf   New York

For the fabulous Janet Schulman
—J.S.

For Isabella Brown
—M.B.

THIS IS A BORZOI BOOK PUBLISHED BY ALFRED A. KNOPF

Text copyright © 2008 by Judy Sierra
Illustrations copyright © 2008 by Marc Brown

Knopf, Borzoi Books, and the colophon are registered trademarks of Random House, Inc.

Published in the United States by Alfred A. Knopf,
an imprint of Random House Children's Books,
a division of Random House, Inc., New York.

Library of Congress Cataloging-in-Publication Data
Sierra, Judy.
Born to read / by Judy Sierra ; illustrated by Marc Brown. — 1st ed.
p.   cm.
Summary: A little boy named Sam discovers the many unexpected ways in
which a love of reading can come in handy, and sometimes even save the day.
ISBN 978-0-375-84687-8 (trade) — ISBN 978-0-375-94687-5 (lib. bdg.)
[1. Books and reading—Fiction. 2. Reading—Fiction. 3. Stories in rhyme.]
I. Brown, Marc Tolon, ill. II. Title.
PZ8.3.S577Bor 2008   [E]—dc22   2007002306

The illustrations in this book were created using gouache on wood.

MANUFACTURED IN CHINA
August 2008
10 9 8 7 6 5 4 3 2 1

First Edition

In the town of Sunny Skies,
A tiny baby blinked his eyes
At dragons dancing overhead
And letters painted on his bed.

"That's me!" he thought. "My name is Sam.
I'm born to read. I know I am."

Sam flashed his mom a hopeful look.
She opened up a picture book,
Then another,
Then another,
Then another,
Then another.

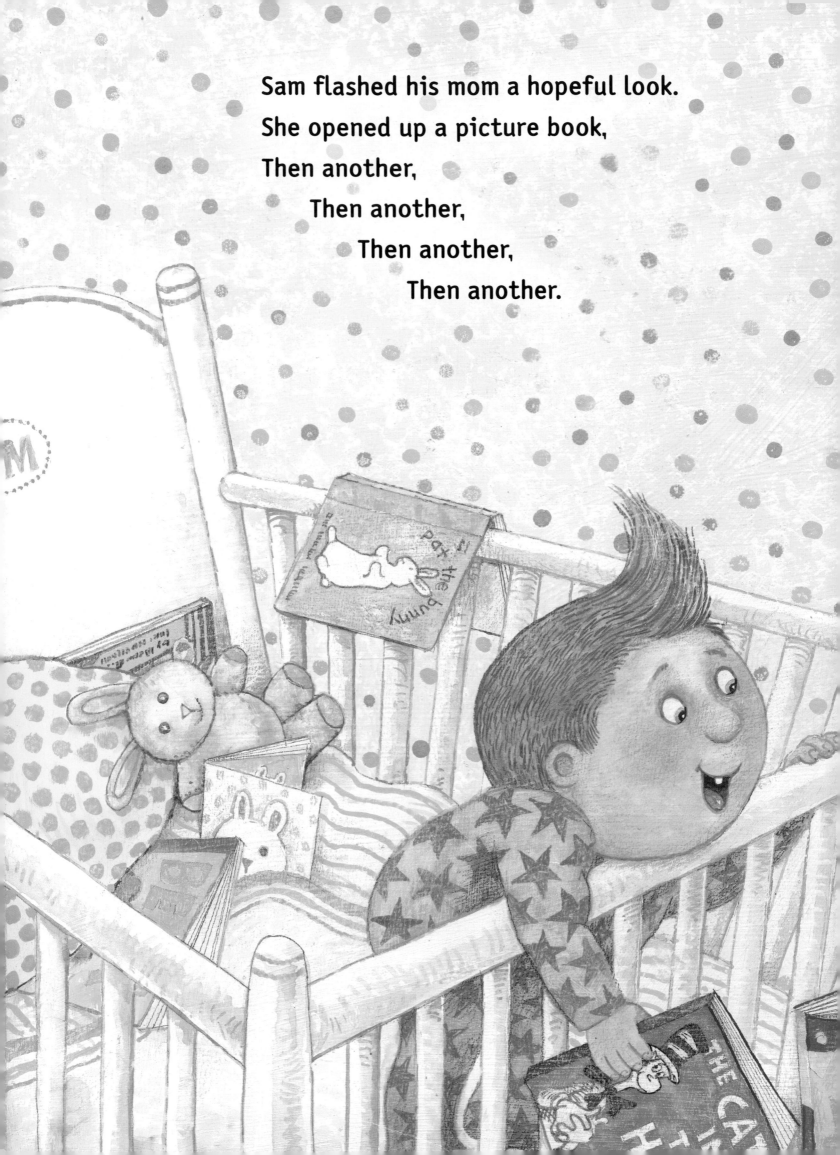

Such a perfect, patient mother!

Sam became a
reading
star.

He helped his papa drive the car.

He helped his sisters do their chores.

Please mop the floor. Love, Mom

He helped himself at grocery stores.

Once, when Sam was almost four,
His knees turned green, his thumbs got sore,
His cheeks were flecked with yellow spots.

They rushed him off to Doctor Potts,
Who cried,

"It's Martian Mustard-ation.
You will need an operation!"

Sam asked, "Is that necessary?
Let me see that dictionary.
Here's a better diagnosis:

Harmless Preschool
Play-dough-osis."

Sam read in bed,

and in the hall,

and in the tub,

and at the mall.

He read while playing basketball.

Passing by the Pizza Place,
Sam spied a poster: CYCLE RACE!

Sam read books on
motivation,
concentration,
muscle action,
getting traction,

BIKE REPAIR

good nutrition,
grand ambition,
playing fair,
and bike repair.

On Saturday at half past nine,
As Sam approached the starting line,
All the racers roared with laughter.
They would not be laughing after
Sam took off at lightning speed
And sprinted to an early lead—
Uphill, downhill, like a rocket,
Stopping once to fix a sprocket.

When the pack was lost from view,
Sam paused to read a poem or two,
Popped a wheelie just for fun,
And finished up as number one.
"Here's my secret," Sam decreed.
"Readers win and winners read."

One dark December afternoon,
The baby giant, Grundaloon,
Came slowly stomping through Sam's town—
He turned the playground upside down—
Kicking buckets, squashing balls,
Grabbing teddy bears and dolls.
And since he was a truck-sized lout,
No grown-ups dared to call
"Time out!"

When Grundaloon had lurched away,

The townsfolk cried,

"He's gone! Hooray!"

"But what if he comes back . . . ?" Sam wondered.

"Think of all the things he plundered."

Sam gathered picture books and snacks
And traced the naughty giant's tracks,
Around the lake, across the bridge,
And found him resting on a ridge.

"Fee, fie, fo, fum," the giant said.
"I'll grind your books to make my bread."
"No, no," said Sam. "Have cake instead.
Let's read about a silly cat,
A caterpillar getting fat,
An alphabet that climbs a tree,
A friendly aardvark from TV."
Grundaloon smiled sleepily.
He sighed and sipped a cup of tea.
And while the giant ate his snack up,
Sam discreetly called for backup.

Responding to Sam's SOS,
A cargo jet from UPS
Transported Grundaloon, express,
Back to his mommy giantess.

Sam hustled home with sacks of toys
For all the waiting girls and boys.
Then everyone began to sing,
**"Yes, readers can
do anything!"**

One point remains a mystery:
Just what will Sam grow up to be?

A baseball player?
A city mayor?
A firefighter?
A mystery writer?
A movie actor?
A chiropractor?
A statistician?
A rock musician?

TIME

PULITZER
PRIZE GOES
TO SAM
Read all about it!

Sunny Skies
vening New
Sam rocks!
BASEBALL
STARS
FIREFIGHTER
HEROES

Sam has not decided yet.
Perhaps he'll be an astro-vet
With offices in outer space.
**Yes, readers can
go anyplace!**